CHRISTMAS IN LAKE CHELAN

A LAKE CHELAN NOVELLA

SHIRLEY PENICK

CHRISTMAS IN LAKE CHELAN

Contact me:

www.shirleypenick.com

www.facebook.com/ShirleyPenickAuthor

To sign up for Shirley's Monthly Newsletter, sign up on my website or send email to shirleypenick@outlook.com, subject newsletter.

CHAPTER ONE

Theodore Beaumont-Jordan's eyes were glued out the window on the view, as the helicopter pilot slowly cruised over the mountains and down to the small town, that he still felt was home. He'd spent his first sixteen years in the mountains surrounding the tiny town of Chedwick, Washington. The town had grown since the first day he'd stepped foot into it.

The amusement park, art gallery, and wedding venue had brought renewed life to the town that had been on the brink of extinction nine years ago. The web designer that had moved to town, after the forest fire that had driven a young, frightened, and ignorant Ted to town, had done a wonderful job of showcasing the many artisans and businesses in the remote village.

Ted knew the fire had caused a lot of damage, but it had saved him from a life of loneliness, and had given him back his family. He shook himself mentally and pulled his thoughts away from what might have happened, if he hadn't been driven into town.

This was a day for good thoughts, he'd convinced his

mother to spend the holidays in the Lake Chelan valley. He couldn't wait to see everyone. He'd not been back in several years and he wanted to see all the people and their families. So many babies had been born since he'd last been here, he loved little kids. He had a subscription to the town newspaper and also kept up with the goings on posted on social media.

His mother spoke, pulling his attention from the view, "It is a quaint little town, it will be good for family vacations."

Rebecca Davenport tensed, hiding her sneer from his mother by pretending an interest in the town. "Boarding school and the French Riviera maybe," she muttered before turning back to his mother. "Quite right, Momma B."

His mother beamed her satisfaction. He couldn't for the life of him, figure out why his mother didn't see Rebecca's, never Becky, God forbid, true colors. He'd allowed his mother to invite Rebecca along, hoping it would open his mother's eyes to the fact that he and Rebecca would never suit.

He didn't like her cold, selfish, judgmental attitude, and she didn't like him. Rebecca did like his name, his money, and the company he was working day and night, learning to run.

His mother hoped for an engagement this Christmas. Not happening if he had anything to say about it.

The helicopter landed on their private pad with a gentle thump. Rebecca snarled. "Theodore, you really must find a better pilot, this one about jars my teeth out of my head with each landing."

His mother laughed. "Rebecca you are such a tender thing, to even notice the slight bump. Come along dear and you can have a rest after our journey."

Ted wanted to roll his eyes, he'd heard things about Rebecca and his pilot that made him believe she had it out for the guy. His pilot, apparently, didn't like playing lapdog for spoiled heiress, especially this ones.

Rebecca resting for a while would give him a chance to go into town alone and greet his friends, before subjecting them to her. With fingers crossed he helped the women down the short ramp and into the massive house his mother had built. It could hold half the town. He'd been in awe of it as a teen, but now it seemed like a waste of space and money. Even though he'd been in this world of affluence for nine years, he still had trouble with the extravagance.

TAMARA LYNCH HEARD THE HELICOPTER BEFORE SHE COULD see it. It wasn't the rescue helicopter, or the firefighting ones that had spent so much of the summer flying back and forth over their town nine years ago. No, this was the sleek black one she'd not seen in nearly five years. If it was the same one. She hoped it was, she'd like to see Ted again, the last time he and his mother had visited he'd just grown into his adult height, but was still gangly. He'd been less awkward, but still not fully confident in his role in life.

Far different from the first time she'd seen him. Dressed in buckskins, dirty, eating with his hands. She'd been shocked by his manners, but had noticed him glancing around the restaurant and copying other people's behavior. By the end of the meal he'd used his fork a couple of times for the salad and also wiped his hands and mouth on the napkin. Later, rumors had spread that he'd been kidnapped by his father as a baby, and he'd spent his entire life camping in the mountains above their town.

He'd come back every year for the first few years, his mother had built a beautiful mansion outside of town and there were still caretakers living there, even though they hadn't been back in years. The helicopter went directly towards that area and then landed, out of view. She turned and hurried on to her job at that same restaurant she'd started working in at fifteen. Nine years she'd worked there, Amber was a good boss, so she couldn't complain, but she dreamed of opening her own public relations firm, and she would, as soon as she finished her bachelor's degree through the online part of the Washington State University, affectionately known as Wazoo. It wouldn't be long now; she would finish up in the spring semester and graduate in June.

Tammy rushed into the restaurant. "Ted's back. I just saw his helicopter land."

Amber smiled. "It will be good to see him again. I've missed seeing him."

"Me, too. He's always so nice. It's so close to the holidays, do you think he'll stick around for them?"

"Time will tell," Amber said.

Tammy clocked in and started doing her opening shift chores. After the breakfast rush they had to refill everything for the lunch crowd.

Tammy noticed a tall well-built man enter the restaurant, he wore slacks and a button-up shirt, a tie hung loosely around his neck. It had to be Ted. His thick brown hair was short but with a tiny bit of wave over his forehead. His blue eyes sparkled with his typical exuberance for life, although there was a tiny bit of caution or something that dimmed that joy. She supposed that came with maturity and living in the real world.

She felt herself drift toward where he stood. He was a fine-looking man and she felt like she was caught in a tractor beam.

CHAPTER TWO

Ted grinned when he walked into Amber's restaurant, his mother and Rebecca were having a salad for lunch and then resting. That left him free to eat a hamburger at Amber's, it had been his first meal in the real world, where he or his father had not killed the meat and cooked it. It was a special memory, the fact that he'd eaten his salad with his fingers made him want to cringe, but he'd not known any better, so he let it go.

Amber was out front, and he walked right up to her and lifted her in a bear hug, twirling her around.

She laughed, "Ted, it's so good to have you back in town."

"It's good to be back, Amber. You're my first stop, I must have one of your hamburgers, with salad and French fries."

Amber grinned. "Tammy, you heard the man. Do you want something to drink?"

"Just water, I have never gotten a taste for anything else. I have wine once in a while to appease my mother, but water is my drink of choice." He looked over at the waitress hovering nearby, she was a gorgeous woman and something about her reminded him of the busgirl that had worked for Amber years ago. He went with his gut that this was the same person. "Tammy, it's good to see you again. You've grown into a lovely woman."

Tammy blushed and stammered, "You've grown up yourself."

He thought back to what he'd looked like at sixteen. Long ragged hair, crooked teeth, buckskin britches and moccasins, and a Lake Chelan t-shirt he'd stolen from a tourist shop. He chuckled at the comparison between the boy he'd been and the man he was now, in his designer suits and Italian loafers. "That happens. It's been a few years."

Tammy smiled and then turned to go, muttering, "I'll get your order in." Then she peeked back over her shoulder and with a little sass showing in her eyes, said, "I assume you'd like a fork this time."

He burst out laughing. "Yes, please. I even know how to use one now."

He watched her walk away with a sassy strut, God, she was sexy as hell. When she was out of sight he turned back to Amber. "So, did I hear correctly that you have a two-year-old son?"

"You did, and just to catch you up on the gossip, we are expecting a daughter next summer."

Joy flooded him at her news. "Congratulations. That's wonderful."

Tammy was going to hide out in the back for a minute or two while the cook got Ted's lunch ready, she was overwhelmed by just how hot he'd become, she'd had to fight to keep calm and collected, when what she really wanted to do was rub up against him like a cat.

He'd grown at least six inches and filled out; he'd been muscular as a teen from living on the land and from the rock sculptures he made. He'd called them his rocks and had left some in lieu of payment for the things he'd stolen to stay alive. The detailed, gorgeous sculptures had sold for way more than what he'd taken. She'd heard his father was a no-account sculptor and had taught his son the basics, and then Ted had taken it to a level that far surpassed his father's work.

Now his body was filled out, there were still plenty of muscles, but they fit his frame. He'd had some orthodontic work done and his teeth were straight and white. The business clothes made him look powerful. She supposed if he was running the family business it was necessary, he was only twenty-five and running a major transportation corporation.

What an amazing man to go from living off the grid to where he was today. He didn't seem the least bit jaded or bitter or snooty. Just a regular guy, albeit in designer clothes and shoes. She chuckled and gathered silverware, made him a salad and grabbed a large glass of iced water.

She slid his food onto the table in front of him. "Here you go, Ted."

"Thanks, Tammy."

"Is there anything else I can get you? Your burger should be out in a minute."

He glanced around the mostly empty restaurant. "I was wondering if I could ask you a few questions. Do you have time?"

"Sure, I just came on shift, so you're my first customer." She could finish her shift prep work later. There wasn't much left, anyway. "What questions?"

"We're going to be here through the holidays, so I want to know what kinds of things might be happening around town."

She grinned. "Nothing big and elaborate. The school has a holiday pageant, it embraces all the holidays, both in America and around the world. Each class gets to pick what holiday they want to depict, so it's always a hodge-podge. They have it the last night before winter break. The only thing you can count on is the third-grade class always does a live nativity. They've had that role for somewhere around sixty years."

"That sounds like fun. What else?"

"Carol Anderson has an open house at her bed and breakfast, with all kinds of snacks and drinks. It's very festive and nearly the whole town shows up at one time or another."

"Mayor Carol?"

"She stepped down from being mayor when she opened the bed and breakfast. Hmm, now let me think, what else. Oh. Hank has hayrides between Thanksgiving and Christmas, one of the things Ellen talked him into doing. They always have hot chocolate and lots of cookies, because Ellen and the kids like to bake."

"Aren't the kids teenagers?"

"Beth is sixteen, she just started driving, the twins just hit their teen years, so they try to act cool, but they still love it. A tradition is a tradition." She wondered if he had family traditions, he'd missed so much of that. It made her sad to think about it.

"One more thing, the library has a reading of *The Night Before Christmas* on Christmas eve, everyone wears Christmas sweaters and Santa hats. Then for New Years, there's a town gathering at Greg's bar for a party."

"Those all sound like fun, thanks Tammy."

"If I hear of anything else, I'll make a point to let you know."

"That's great. Maybe we should exchange phone numbers so you can text me."

She didn't normally give out her phone number, but in this case she would. She might just sit and stare at the contact and dream silly dreams.

CHAPTER THREE

After finishing his lunch, Ted made the rounds of the other people in town he wanted to visit. The art gallery was his next stop where Kristen and Mary Ann greeted him with joy, both had been instrumental in his mother finding him.

"Ted, we didn't know you were coming to town." Mary Ann hugged him so hard he couldn't draw a breath. "Are you staying long? We just got your newshipment of sculptures. People love them."

After disengaging from the effervescent Mary Ann, Kristen gave him a much more reticent hug. For her introverted self, it was huge.

"I'll be here until after the New Year. I talked my mom into coming for the whole season. Tammy gave me a list of events the town holds. I want to see everyone's babies, too."

Mary Ann clapped her hands. "Yay! That's six weeks to enjoy you. The best place to see all the kids is the holiday pageant the school puts on. We all go whether we have children old enough to participate or not."

"Already on my list."

Mary Ann chattered on for a few more minutes until a customer came in, then she was off to take care of them.

Kristen said, "It's great to have you in town, Ted. Come by any time."

Next, he went by the jail and chatted with the police chief and the dispatcher, Michelle. He visited his cell, it had been the first real bed he'd ever slept in, that he could remember anyway. The toilet had been a real marvel, and the sink, he'd never seen either of them before. Michelle had made sure he had plenty of food, while he'd spent the few days in jail, before his mother had made restitution for the things he'd stolen, to survive. He'd thought the jail cell was the lap of luxury back then. He almost missed those days of innocence.

He drove around town to see all the growth and renovations. It looked to him like the economy was booming. A far cry from what it had been. When he'd had his fill, he drove back to the house to tell his mom and Rebecca about the fun things that were planned in town.

Rebecca sneered. "Christmas cookies, after the school holiday pageant? That's the most this town has to offer? When we could be at the Nutcracker in New York or Moscow?"

His mother laughed. "Now Rebecca, that's something that can be done any year. We're embracing a small-town Holiday season this year."

Ted wasn't sure he should continue with his list. "There are hayrides at the ranch between Thanksgiving and Christmas, and the library has a reading of *The Night before Christmas*."

His phone chimed and as he looked at the text, he heard Rebecca mutter "Oh, Joy."

He smiled to see the text was from Tammy. She'd thought of a couple more activities.

"Looks like there is also a tree lighting ceremony on the

Sunday after Thanksgiving. Closer to Christmas there are carolers strolling the shopping area."

Rebecca stood back stiffly, with her arms folded, staring out the window.

So, he spoke to his mom. "On New Year's Eve, everyone gathers at Greg's bar for a party."

Rebecca whirled around. "New Year's Eve!" she screeched. "You want to stay that long in this backwater town, and eat fucking cookies? We always go to the rooftop restaurant at the Marriott Marquis to watch the Time Square ball drop."

Of course, she did, she wouldn't want to go down into the actual Times Square with the rest of humanity. Ted shrugged. "That was the plan, Rebecca."

His mom looked uncomfortable at Rebecca's outburst.

His phone chimed again. This time Tammy was telling him about the pancake breakfast the Fire Department put on for New Year's Day. He grinned but decided not to mention that.

"Ted, who are you getting texts from?" his mother asked.

"Tammy from Amber's restaurant. I asked her about town events."

Rebecca narrowed her eyes at him and flounced out of the room.

His mom watched her go. "She'll get used to the idea. It's just different for her. Shall we go to Amber's tonight for dinner?"

"Sure, Amber has a very nice fine dining area, that maybe Rebecca will enjoy."

AMBER ASKED, "ARE YOU SURE YOU CAN HANDLE A SECOND shift tonight?"

Tammy was tired and wanted off her feet, but they were short one server tonight in the fine dining section of the restaurant and Tammy had her uniform for that side in her locker. "Sure, not a problem. I'd just like to put my feet up for a few minutes, if that's all right."

"Oh, by all means take an hour now. Use my office, I'll have some food sent in so you can eat, too. What would you like?"

Tammy thought back to Ted's enjoyment of his burger. She didn't eat like that often but today she couldn't think of anything else. "A cheeseburger with French fries and a side salad."

"Go ahead on back, use the couch to take a little rest. It shouldn't be busy tonight, but you never know. It seems like everyone in town gets a hankering at the same time."

Tammy laughed. "Ain't that the truth?"

She went back and stretched out on the couch in Amber's office. She'd texted Ted a couple of times with other activities she'd thought of, but he'd not responded. *Guess he's too busy being a billionaire to bother with little hometown girls like me.* With a sigh she laid the phone on the table next to the couch and let herself doze.

What seemed like seconds later, but was actually about twenty minutes, Amber brought her in the hamburger she'd asked for. "Stay right there, I have a rolling tray like they have at hospitals, so you can keep your feet up while you eat. I used it a lot when I was preggers."

After she ate Tammy washed up in the bathroom, put on her nicer uniform, and was ready for her second shift.

An hour into her shift Ted walked in. Not the easy-going friendly man from this morning. This was the powerhouse billionaire, he was dressed in a charcoal gray suit with pinstripes, a crisp white shirt, and red power tie. His mother and another woman accompanied him.

Tammy remembered his mother as being kind, and so grateful to be getting her son back, she'd been sweet to everyone. The other woman was a willowy blond, gorgeous, in a dress that would probably cost Tammy an entire year's salary, and Christian Louboutin shoes. She was gorgeous, but as Tammy looked in her eyes there was a coldness that made her want to shiver.

Ted was seated in her section. She didn't know if that was good or bad. But she walked over. Before she could say a word, Ted shot to his feet, and took her arm. "Mother this is Tammy. Tammy, this is my mother, Lenore Beaumont-Jordan."

Lenore smiled. "You've been sending Ted texts about town activities. That's so nice of you."

"Thank-you, Ted is special to our town and we want him to enjoy his time here during the holidays."

Ted beamed and then turned toward the other woman. "Rebecca, this is Tammy. Tammy this is my... um... friend, Rebecca Davenport."

With no acknowledgment of the introduction, Rebecca asked, "Are you our server for the evening?"

"Yes, I am, it's a pleasure to meet you."

"Do you have any decent champagne?"

Tammy recoiled at the coldness in the woman's voice, but pulled out the wine list and gave it to the woman. "Why, yes, we have two splendid varieties."

"Two?" she rolled her eyes.

Ted said tightly, "There only needs to be one, since we'll only be drinking one." He looked over Rebecca's shoulder and ordered the best.

Tammy turned to go, obviously dismissed.

Rebecca said, "Tina, I need a new place setting. I see a water spot."

"Tammy, her name is Tammy," Ted said.

Tammy smiled at him and removed the place setting. "I'll be right back. But before I go, we have locally sourced blackened salmon on special tonight in a white wine reduction sauce, with fingerling potatoes and steamed broccoli."

She returned a few minutes later with the new place setting for the queen. The champagne and flutes. The busboy followed her out with the ice stand. After expertly removing the stopper she poured them each a flute of the bubbly beverage.

"Are you ready to order?"

Ted and his mother nodded. Rebecca said, "Give us another few minutes, Theresa."

Tammy fought to keep her temper, the woman was deliberately calling her the wrong name and making more work. She moved on to her next table, trying not to let Rebecca get under her skin.

She was on the way to the kitchen to place the other table's order, when Rebecca said loudly, "Theodora, we're ready to order now."

With silent apologies to the other table she stopped to take their orders. Ted and his mother both ordered quickly with no fuss. Rebecca, on the other hand, had to modify every part of her meal. She ordered the salmon special, but she wanted the sauce on the side. She didn't want potatoes, but she didn't want two servings of broccoli, what else did they have? After Tammy running through all the other vegetable options, Rebecca chose the potatoes.

Tammy wanted to roll her eyes but remained professional. "Oh, and Tiana, can you please bring my fiancé a fresh glass of water?"

With a quick glance at Ted, who'd turned bright red, Tammy went off to do the woman's bidding.

He was engaged? To that witch? Poor Ted. Men could be

so clueless about things like Rebecca was pulling. All they saw was the willowy sophisticated blond.

The rest of the evening dragged as she served their table. Rebecca never once called her by the right name. The other tables were in and out, but Rebecca seemed to be dragging out the time spent.

Ted finally asked for the check and she heard Rebecca say, "But it's still early, darling, I'm sure Taylor doesn't mind."

Tammy couldn't hear his reply, but he didn't look happy.

Ted took the check and quickly signed it. Then dragged Rebecca out of her chair. While he helped his mother, Rebecca turned to her with a smirk. "Have a nice life, Twinkletoes."

Tammy wanted to slap that smirk right off her face, but she smiled sweetly and said, "You too, Rapunzel."

When they were gone and she turned in the sales receipt, she was horrified to see Ted had left her a hundred-dollar tip. Was he rubbing her nose in his wealth? Apologizing for his bitchy fiancé? Or what? She didn't want to think about it, so she cleaned up, closed out and took her tired butt home.

Where all she did was think about Rebecca, the tip, and Ted.

ed was mortified at Rebecca's actions. The woman had done everything in her power to make Tammy feel bad, calling her all those stupid names, fussing over every tiny thing. But the worst was her calling him her fiancé, he'd seen Tammy withdraw, from that moment on. He didn't know what to say or do, so he'd left a huge tip and hoped he could see Tammy again to explain. This wasn't something he could clean up over a text message.

He was not Rebecca's fiancé and after her display in the restaurant, he never would be. She was always rude to people she felt were below her on the social ladder, but she'd been horrendous to Tammy.

He planned to talk to her as soon as they got back to the house. Set her straight on the engagement lie, confront her about her snooty attitude, and offer her the helicopter to return home.

Before the front door was completely closed, Rebecca said, "I'm so tired. I'm going straight to bed. See you both in the morning." Then she nearly ran up the stairs away from him.

His mom watched her go then turned to him, eyes bright with enthusiasm. "I didn't know you and Rebecca were engaged, when did this happy occurrence take place?"

With a huge sigh he said, "It didn't. We're not engaged and after her performance tonight we won't be."

His mother's shoulders drooped. "Oh, Teddy. I think she was just tired and feeling cranky."

"Mom, I don't love her, I don't even like her. She's not a nice person."

"Theodore, I want you to listen to me. I married for love and you can see how badly that turned out. It's much better to marry someone in your social status. Rebecca fits that bill nicely. I think you can teach her how to be kinder. She's still young."

"But, mom…"

"No, now you just give this relationship time. I think after a few days here you'll see a change in her."

He didn't like that idea one bit. He was ready to call his pilot and send her on her way. But maybe his mom was right, she had loved his dad and his dad had turned out to be a mean, vindictive jerk. "All right, I'll give it a chance."

She kissed his cheek. "That's all I ask. Goodnight, darling."

As his mother went up the stairs to her room, he thought about how Tammy had wilted when Rebecca had announced she was his fiancé. But then she'd carried on and was kind and accommodating. Now that was the kind of person he'd like to marry, someone who put others first.

As that idea continued to swirl around in his head, he realized there was a lot more to Tammy that he enjoyed. He would like the chance to get to know her better, but with Rebecca in tow, he didn't see how that could happen. Dammit, sometimes it was hard to do the 'right' thing.

TAMMY MANAGED TO AVOID TED AND HIS BITCHY FIANCÉ BY swapping shifts with one of the early morning servers. She'd used the excuse of needing to study for her exams. She normally studied in the mornings when her mind was fresh and she absorbed things faster, but she'd be happy to work harder to not have to see Ted and that woman. How someone as nice as Ted, could be engaged to someone so mean, she had no idea.

Tammy had first thought that maybe it was just she that Rebecca was a snot to, but she'd heard differently. Every waitress hated her and couldn't wait until she left town. She also heard that Ted was leaving enormous tips, so she chalked it up as his way of apologizing and put the money in her bank account rather than returning it, which had been her first plan.

When Kristen slammed in the door and stomped over to a table Tammy got her first look at the fact that Rebecca wasn't only mean to servers.

"Hi Kristen, what can I get you?"

"A huge mug of coffee with many, many refills and pancakes. I need pancakes after dealing with that bitch. Oh, and my sister will be here shortly for the same, because Ted took her over there, after she sneered at everything in my art gallery."

"Everything? Surely not your jewelry, or the glass?"

"Oh yes, she did, and I quote, 'Obviously these are inferior works that should have been tossed. Instead she's sending them to this backwater town where no one will recognize it.' The bitch. Nolan just laughed when I told him what she'd said about his mother's art."

Kristen took her knife and tapped the table with it like she was stabbing someone in her mind. "And my jewelry was juvenile and okay for everyday wear, but nothing she could possibly wear out to a Broadway play. Ted saw me getting ready to clobber her with one of the glass sculptures and dragged her to my sister's boutique."

Tammy sagged at that; Kristen's sister sold one of a kind wedding dresses. "Probably to choose a wedding dress, they're engaged you know."

Kristen frowned then shook her head. "No, I don't think so. First there is no engagement ring on her finger and second Ted acts like he can barely tolerate her. Even his mother didn't like her actions. After Ted dragged the rude witch next door, Lenore stayed and bought two sculptures and several pieces of my jewelry, calling it wearable art, and that it was certainly exquisite enough for Broadway. No, I don't think they are engaged and if they are, it won't last long, he's too nice of a guy to put up with her venom."

As she went to put in the orders, Tammy hoped with all her heart that Kristen was right. Not that Ted would ever look at her to be in his life, but just because she hated the thought of him tied to such a self-centered person. He deserved someone sweet and loving. And if her heart yearned to be chosen for that role, she just hid that deep down, knowing it could never be.

CHAPTER FIVE

He'd had enough. Ted didn't care what his mother thought, he was confronting Rebecca today. He wasn't about to let her ruin his holiday here in Chedwick. She'd already trashed Thanksgiving. They'd been invited to the family dinner at the Bed and Breakfast run my former-mayor Carol. It had been a lovely affair with excellent food and a fun atmosphere, all except for one notable exception, Rebecca.

She'd turned her nose up at the food, and talked about the all-day Thanksgiving buffet at one of her favorite New York restaurants, where there was caviar and champagne, the turkey carefully hidden in puff pastry and the cranberry sauce turned into a Champagne drizzle. She'd deliberately called each family member by the wrong name, then insulted each one with some dig. He'd been ready to slap her, and he wasn't the violent sort.

When they'd finally left, he'd breathed a sigh of relief, later it turned to fury at the thought of what a pleasant day it could have been if Rebecca had not been with them. His mother had tried to gently point out that she'd embarrassed the family, but Rebecca had only laughed and said they needed thicker skin.

He had his helicopter pilot doing his flight check, he was putting Rebecca on it as soon as he could.

His mother came down and found him waiting at the foot of the stairs. "Ted, whatever are you doing hovering here?"

"Mother, I've given her a chance and cannot stand it any longer. I'm putting Rebecca on the helicopter as soon as she appears."

His mom sucked in a breath, but he didn't let her speak. He took her arm and led her into the sitting room. Guiding her to a chair he knelt in front of her and took her hands in his. "Mom, I know you said I should marry within my class, that I should give her a chance. But I think you're looking at my life through a false view of your own. I know you married dad for love, but I don't think dad married you for the same reason. I think he married you for the class, for the prestige, and maybe for the money."

Tears filled her eyes, but he went on, he had to, this was too important. "When your father saw what a lazy bum he was, and didn't hand him over the company, I think dad was angry. I think he let that anger fester until after I was born and weaned, then he 'paid back that old bastard and his daughter' by kidnapping me. I never understood what he meant by that phrase, but he muttered it often over the years."

"Oh, Teddy, I didn't realize."

"I know Mom, and I never told you. When I finally realized that you were the daughter it all clicked for me, but I didn't want to hurt you by telling you. He didn't allow me to use the word mother. If I did, he'd tell me it was a bad word and give me a thrashing. Nolan is the one that finally told me the truth."

"I know, Nolan told me how you flinched when he said

the word. I didn't want to hurt your feelings by mentioning how much it pained me to see what your father had done."

"I think Rebecca is cut from the same cloth as my father, Mom."

Lenore blinked back tears and firmed her expression. "You might be right. Do what your heart tells you, Ted. It's led you down the right path all along. I love you, Son."

"I love you too, Mother."

Two hours later, mother and son stood on the helipad, arm in arm, to watch Rebecca go back to the city. Ted had been firm, but kind, when he'd told her they had no future. Rebecca had screamed and thrown things, every filthy word in her vocabulary had been tossed at his head, his mother, and his town.

They both breathed a sigh of relief when the helicopter was out of sight. Ted knew he would need to give his pilot a hazard duty bonus. Poor guy. Fortunately, Ted had booked her a private jet out of Wenatche, so his pilot wouldn't need to tolerate her too long. Still, hazard duty pay was in order.

Tammy stopped in her tracks when she heard the helicopter. Was Ted leaving? Had he knuckled under to his horrible fiancé's wishes and gone back to take her to The Nutcracker and all the other things she was accustomed to? Their small-town offerings were probably foolish in her eyes. She watched the helicopter fly swiftly out of town and wished them all well.

With a sigh she walked into her small apartment, she had one more final exam before the winter break. She was going to be off work for the next few days to prepare for it.

The last day of the week, Tammy showered and dressed, she'd finished her final and was ready to get out of her apartment, she'd been cooped up for days. She needed to see her friends and neighbors. Tonight, was the school holiday pageant and everyone would be there.

The live nativity was so darling this year. They held it outside before the rest of the pageant took place in the auditorium. She wished Ted could have seen it, he would have loved it. As if she'd conjured him with her thoughts, he materialized at her side.

"Ted, what are you doing here? I thought I saw your helicopter leave a few days ago.

"Yeah it did, Rebecca wanted to go back to New York for the holidays thatshe's accustomed to."

That was certainly a relief, everyone in town would have a better holiday without her being here. "I'm sorry, Ted. I'm sure you'll miss your fiancé during the holidays."

"I'm not sorry, I'm glad. Rebecca and I are not engaged, and never have been. I don't know why she said that."

Tammy's heart sped up; he wasn't engaged? Maybe…no, they weren't in the same class, he would never—

He interrupted her downward spiraling thoughts. "I was wondering if I could, um, sit with you during the pageant and maybe take you out afterward, for a drink or a meal."

Was he asking her out on a date? Tonight? Joy filled her, but she couldn't, not tonight. She shook her head and watched sadness fill his eyes. He looked down, so she couldn't see his expression. That gave her even more hope. "I can't go out tonight, I have to work the early shift tomorrow. But you can sit with me now and I'm free tomorrow afternoon or evening, we could go out then."

His head shot up. "Tomorrow? Awesome."

Ted was on cloud nine. He spent the rest of the evening with Tammy, watching the holiday pageant, laughing out loud at some of the antics. After the last class performed, they all moved to the cafeteria for cookies and fruit punch. While the fruit punch was nothing special, the cookies were delicious, the bakery in town, Warm Buns, had supplied them. The owner had made all kinds of cookies in the shapes of all the holidays that had been in the pageant. He guessed she'd had to do some research to find appropriate designs for some of the obscure international holidays the kids had chosen to depict.

As they ate cookies and drank punch, they talked to their friends and neighbors and Ted got to meet all the children that had been born since he'd moved out of town. His mother was making the rounds chatting with everyone, especially one older man, whom he thought worked at the pharmacy.

It was a perfect night and he had a date with Tammy tomorrow.

CHAPTER SIX

ammy rushed home after her shift at the restaurant, eager to get cleaned up for her date with Ted. Nothing could come of it, with the two of them living on opposite coasts, but she was going to enjoy him while he was in town. She was dying to get to know him better. She'd like to hear all about his transition from living in isolation to joining a very powerful family.

She scurried into the shower to wash the work scents off and shave everywhere, she didn't know if they would get anywhere near the bedroom, but she would rather be ready and have it not happen, than the alternative.

She was going to wear something flirty but also warm. It was winter and chilly out.

Tammy decided on black slacks and an ultra-feminine yellow top with long sleeves that showed off her assets. A cozy sweater would keep her warm, rather than a coat. She slipped her feet into booties with a three-inch heel, just high enough to make her ass look great, but not too high for a stroll.

She left her makeup understated, just smoky eyes,

mascara and lip-gloss with a hint of color. A spritz of her favorite perfume and she was ready for anything. Except waiting. She wasn't a fan of waiting.

Rather than pacing, she checked her online classes to see if her grades had come in. It was doubtful, since she'd just finished finals, but some professors were speedy. Apparently not the ones she had this semester, since there was no change in her scores. Just the old ones staring at her, cursor blinking. She shut the laptop so it could go to sleep and looked at the time. Not long now.

A final check in the mirror to make sure everything was perfect and then he should be knocking on the door. She nearly skipped to the hall mirror and did a quick spin. No wardrobe casualties that she could see.

She made herself walk sedately toward the door, until she heard the knock and then she rushed to answer it. Ted stood there looking like something out of a GQ magazine, black slacks, cream turtleneck, and black sportscoat. He was so good looking it took her a moment to speak.

"Hi Ted, come on in." She held the door open and he walked in, his scent wafted past her and she wanted to purr. "Did you want to sit for a bit or hit the streets?"

He tilted his head for a moment and then laughed. "Hit the streets, good one. I was thinking of having a late lunch at the pizza place and then an even later dinner, anywhere but Amber's."

She laughed, thrilled he'd planned to spend the whole day with her. "Just because I work there it doesn't mean I don't appreciate the food. But I wouldn't mind steering clear of it tonight."

"How about the Korean Barbecue place? There aren't a lot of restaurants and I don't really feel like bar food. Do you?"

She shook her head. "No, deep fried everything, doesn't really appeal to me."

"Korean Barbecue it is."

❦

TED WAS ENCHANTED BY TAMMY. SHE WAS SO FUN AND OPEN, happy to talk about every subject under the sun. For a small-town girl she was exceptionably knowledgeable. He'd mentioned a minor issue he was having at his company and she had given him several solid suggestions.

"So just how did you become so keen on everything?"

She blushed. "I've always been a news hound. You're going to think I'm weird, but I subscribe to several online newspapers. My degree will be in public relations."

His eyebrows shot up at that statement and he tried to wipe the surprise off his face. "How did you get started on that path?"

Tammy turned bright red at his question, and he wondered why she was so completely embarrassed.

Finally, she took a deep breath and let it out slowly. "You. You started me on the path."

"Me?"

"Yes, after you'd been found and your mother contacted some people were in Amber's, gossiping, as people do. Anyway, they didn't notice me over at the next table bussing the dishes. Bus people aren't very noticeable, which is by design. So, they were talking about how your mom had tried to find you and how you were from this big important family, and it made me curious.

"So, I went to the library and the librarian, Patty Anne, showed me how to research. Twenty-five years ago, when you were kidnapped, nothing much was online, and little had been done, even nine years ago, to put past information online. It taught me a useful skill and gave me a love for journalism."

Her eyes sparkled with enthusiasm and shivers ran through him to see it. All he could say was, "Wow."

"I don't want to be a reporter and see all the gory and horrendous details in the world, but public relations are exciting, to me. How to give people the facts but emphasize the parts that are good for a company or person involved. Bad stuff happens, but how to keep it from being a nightmare that has a life of its own, is what I like. Plus, Chedwick has no PR and could use some, good, bad or ugly. None is worse than bad."

"They probably have some overlap from the game company."

"Sure, but we need more. The town is thriving, but we want to keep it that way and I have ideas about how to go about that."

He smiled and took her hand giving it a little squeeze. "Good for you. I love your excitement and I'm sure you'll be awesome at it."

"Thanks, just one semester to go. Having one of the top-rated colleges nearby with an online program has made it a lot easier. I couldn't take a full load, so it's taken me longer than many others, but that's just life."

He sat there with her warm soft hand in his and decided this was a perfect place to be. Life was pretty darn good.

CHAPTER SEVEN

Tammy was disappointed that Ted hadn't given her a good night kiss last night, other than a peck on the cheek. He'd held her hand and she could read the interest in his eyes, but nothing had come of it. She'd stewed half the night wondering about it. Was it shyness? Some internal code, like no kissing on first dates, or no kissing the peasants? Was he not interested, and she'd read things all wrong?

She'd called herself five times a fool as she'd tossed and turned. When she'd finally drifted off, her mind had taken her places Ted had not, and she'd had hot dreams. She'd woken achy and unsatisfied, so she was in a cranky mood.

She was still on the stupid morning shift, which did not help her cranky situation one bit. She got dressed, yanked her hair into a ponytail and was off to work. Before she walked into the restaurant, she made herself stop and take three deep breaths and willed the cranky away. She worked in customer service, so she had to be polite and professional.

It was a busy morning which was *not* what she'd expected, with it being only a week until Christmas she was surprised to have a whole table of men that she didn't recognize. They looked like a bunch of rowdy hunters in their camo and heavy coats and boots.

She served them and tried to ignore their uncouth comments and innuendos. She chalked it up to men trying to best each other in the rudeness department. It had happened before, and would likely happen again. Waitresses, it seemed, were fair game.

She was delivering their breakfast and had to lean past one of them who grabbed her and pulled her up next to him. She wished she had the coffee pot so she could 'accidentally' spill some on him, but alas, she had left it at the counter to carry over their breakfasts.

"Excuse me. Let me go."

The dumbass just leered at her. "You're a nice armful, girlie. How about a little smooch?"

She was ready to pick up his plate and hit him over the head with it when the guy yelped and let her go. She hurried out of arm's length and saw Ted with fury in his eyes. She didn't know what he'd done to the guy, but he was rubbing his forearm.

"Leave my girlfriend alone."

The men turned their eyes on Ted in his expensive clothes and she knew he was about to be pummeled.

TED FIGURED THE BEST COURSE OF ACTION WAS TO CHANGE the focus of the men seated at the table. "It looks like you fellas have been hunting. Any luck?"

A big guy with a long beard shook his head. "Nope, we didn't even see a hoofprint."

Ted nodded. "Maybe I can help you with that. Do you have a map of where you were?"

The guy that had grabbed Tammy pulled one out of his

jacket's inner pocket. He unfolded it, still glaring at Ted. Finally, breaking his gaze, the man pointed to a place on the map.

Ted examined it. "Yeah, the animals aren't in that area this time of year. He tapped another spot; they are more likely to be here."

Another guy said, "You don't exactly look like the outdoors type, how would you know that?"

"I lived in those mountains over half my life. We had to know where to find food. Didn't have rifles, so we had to be able to get in close, for a bow and arrow or even a hunting knife. Mind if I join you, and I can show you the best way to find them?"

Beard guy waved at the table.

Ted said, "Tammy, sweetheart, can you grab me a pen and bring me my usual?" He didn't have a usual, but he wanted the men to think there was more of a relationship between Tammy and himself than there actually was. He hoped Tammy would catch on and just bring him anything to eat. It really didn't matter what it was.

"Sure thing, honey." She handed him her pen. "Here, take mine. I'll be right back."

He sighed inwardly; glad she'd picked up on his intentions. Looking back at the men he used her pen to outline where the animals usually went this time of year and the easiest access to that area. Ted just hoped the animals still had their past patterns; he hadn't been in the mountains in almost a decade.

When Tammy set down his plate and a cup of coffee, she kissed him on the cheek which sent tingles throughout his body, though he forced himself to have no reaction. "Thanks, love."

They talked hunting for another half hour as they ate, and

then the guys were off like a shot, to get back to the mountains. He hoped they had good luck.

When they were gone Tammy came back and slumped into the chair next to him. "You did good turning their focus off me and onto hunting."

"I figured part of them harassing you was because they were frustrated from their inability to find game. Although you *are* a pretty little armful."

She giggled and the sound shimmered through him. "And I'll be happy to give you a smooch."

"I'll look forward to it. Want to go out with me this afternoon when you get off work? I need to go by the art gallery and do some Christmas shopping."

She rolled her eyes. "Nothing like waiting until the last minute."

"Oh, I have some things purchased, but might as well buy a few more, give into the local economy."

"That's nice of you. I'd be happy to go shopping."

"Then afterward, I'll buy you some dinner."

She put her hand over his and his blood heated at her touch. "Then maybe we can go back to my place for a smooch or two."

"That would be delightful." He decided it might not hurt to grab a few condoms before he picked her up. He didn't want to presume anything, but he didn't want to go unprepared if she had more in mind than a few kisses. A gentleman was always prepared to give his lady what she wanted.

CHAPTER EIGHT

ammy and Ted had fun at the art gallery. She admired his sculptures, there were some that she absolutely loved. They were so well done, it was like the stone came to life. Then she tried on different jewelry, so he could decide what his mom would like. They sniffed all the lotions and bath products, that were made by a local woman.

Ted asked Tammy's opinion on the glass art sculptures, saying they could use a piece for a particular spot in the entryway to his home in town. He also looked over the gorgeous photography on the walls from both photographers, one that had moved away and one that had moved to town to marry a local guy. Both had coffee table books of the Chelan Valley, he owned one of each.

There were lots of other things to look at, and they laughed often, and had so much fun.

He didn't buy much, only a pair of earrings and some lotion he thought his mom would like.

"After we spent all this time in here that's all you're getting?"

"Yeah, for now, I want to think about it all. I'll come back tomorrow and get what I decide on."

"That makes sense I guess."

"Besides, I'm getting hungry. Aren't you?"

"Now that you mention it, I suppose I am."

He took her hand and they walked to his car. They kept one or maybe two vehicles in town, their house was a bit further out, so it made sense. He opened the door for her, and she slid into the Lexus. It was a lovely car, but she'd been surprised they didn't have something even fancier.

"Where are we going?"

"I decided that I didn't want to take you to Amber's since you work there. And I imagine you eat at all the other restaurants in town pretty often, and we hit those yesterday, so I thought maybe the one at the resort, that has the piano."

She'd only been to the resort once, when it first opened, it wasn't a local's type of place. "That sounds fun. I've never eaten there before."

"Good, then it will be something special."

Something special that would remind her of him when he went back to his real life. She would miss being with him. He was a fun guy. They talked and laughed easily. Even though he was uber rich he never acted snobby or above anyone. She supposed his childhood had something to do with that, still he could have gotten haughty.

He also gave her tingles and she hoped they could explore the physical side of things. He was only going to be here a few weeks, so she didn't want to wait too long. She wanted those kinds of memories of him, too. She would find someone to love and be loved by eventually, she assumed, but so far no one had materialized that interested her, besides Ted, and that wasn't meant to be.

❧

TED WAS HAVING THE BEST TIME HE'D EVER HAD WITH A female. The women he'd met and gone out with before this were so cynical and jaded. Tammy was sweet and they had fun together. He didn't feel like he had to watch every word, monitor every action. He could just be himself; he didn't have to play some role.

He loved his mother and he enjoyed his role in the company, working to make sure they remained relevant and kept the stockholders happy, while at the same time keeping the customers enthusiastic. He'd suggested a few things to the board and staff, and had been pleased when they'd accepted his ideas and had run with them, with good results.

However, he was never quite comfortable in the social side of things. People either toadied to him because of his money or shunned him because of his upbringing. Sometimes he didn't know how to act or which fork to use. How to carry on a proper golf conversation, which included innuendos he knew nothing about.

But Tammy? She didn't expect anything of him except for some fun and since she was a small-town girl, he didn't have to put on airs with her. It was refreshing. The restaurant in the resort was upscale, but not snooty. Since it was a place for tourists, there was no dress code, people walking in from a day at the amusement park or time spent on the lake were their normal customers.

Dinner was great, they chatted and shared food, she'd gotten salmon and he'd selected steak, so they made their own surf and turf. The piano player was nice background noise, until they'd finished eating and he'd noticed some couples dancing on a miniscule dance floor.

"Want to dance?" He asked her, after seeing her interest in the other couples.

"If you want to," she said almost shyly.

"I do, Mom made me learn how to dance, so I could hold my own at charity functions."

Her eyes widened and she shook her head. "I don't really know how to waltz or anything like that."

"I'm also perfectly capable of holding a beautiful woman in my arms and shuffling my feet a little bit."

Tammy blushed. "That's more my style."

He stood and held out his hand. "Come on, pretty lady."

The feel of her in his arms was magical. The two of them fit together like they'd been sculpted from the same stone. Her hair smelled like the flowers that had grown in a meadow near the cabin where he'd lived. As a child, he'd loved running through the flowers, releasing their scent.

Holding her in his arms, breathing in the aroma of her hair, was a much better way to enjoy the fragrance.

They swayed and shuffled around in circles, for three songs. He would have gladly stayed there for hours longer, but the musician announced he was leaving. Ted dropped a fifty into the guy's tip jar and walked his date to their table to gather her purse. He left a generous tip for the waitstaff and they proceeded to his car, hand in hand.

On the drive back he took the lake road, so they could enjoy the stars and the moon reflected there. He didn't want the night to end, but he didn't know if Tammy was working in the morning.

He drove her back to her house and walked her to the door. When they got to her door, he leaned in for a goodnight kiss. He'd meant it to be light and friendly, it started that way, but it quickly turned heated. He wasn't quite sure whether that heat was from his doing, or hers. Maybe both.

They kissed for long minutes the heat and passion building. She wrapped her arms around his neck and moved in close, so he enfolded her in his arms and pulled her to him.

She moaned and he was lost, trapped in the blaze of heat they generated.

She pulled away from him. "Let's go inside where we can be more comfortable."

"You don't need to work tomorrow?"

"No, I'm off, but even if I was, you could still come inside."

He nodded, happy to follow her anywhere. She unlocked the door and they went in. She dropped her purse on the floor and took his hand, leading him past a pretty living room and a cheerful kitchen and down the hall. She opened the door to a bedroom and pulled him inside.

He was surprised by her actions, he'd thought they would do some kissing, on the couch and then he'd go home. Apparently, the gorgeous woman wanted more. He could be on board with that. Thank God, he'd bought some condoms.

When she got him into her room she stopped and looked down. "I'm sorry. I'm being kind of aggressive. It's just that you're only here a few weeks and I want to, um, enjoy you while I have the chance."

He pulled her into his arms and kissed her, bringing the heat back for both of them, when she went soft, he broke the kiss and with his mouth on hers said, "I want to be with you, too. I just didn't want to presume. Especially since I'll only be here a few weeks."

She sighed and looked up at him. "Let's spend that time together. Okay?"

"Absolutely." He kissed her again and as their mouths and tongues danced together, their hands got busy removing clothes, touching skin as it was revealed. Shivers and sparks ran rampant over their bodies. Sighs and moans of delight were the only sounds. When they both were divested of their clothing they drew together again, skin to skin, her softness to his hardness. Her breasts smashed against his chest, her soft stomach cradling his erection. The globes of her ass filling his hands. Everywhere they touched the fires lit and ran along nerves, gathering in the center of their bodies.

He backed her toward the bed, she held on and pulled him along. As if he might leave if she didn't. Which was so far from the truth it would have been laughable, if he'd had any kind of ability to laugh. He didn't, he was too immersed in her.

When they got to the bed, she said, "There are condoms in the drawer. I bought them after we talked yesterday."

"I bought some yesterday, too. I'll bet the drugstore was wondering why there was a run on them."

She giggled again, sending fire racing along his veins. "It's Christmas, I imagine they always have a run this time of year."

"You could be right." He reached into the drawer, which was now closer than his wallet, where he'd placed a strip, and pulled out a little foil packet. She climbed onto the bed while he rolled it on and joined her.

He went back to kissing her, while his hands roamed her body, gently squeezing her breasts and causing the nipples to furl, then running his thumb over the tips. She squirmed and moaned at the action. He let his mouth replace his hand and he drew those sensitive nipples, one at a time, into his mouth and suckled.

While he enjoyed her breasts and the moans that elicited, he ran his hand down her body, to between her legs, to find her wet and ready for him. He parted her flesh to reach for the nub hidden there and proceeded to guarantee she was as wet as could be. It didn't take long for her to tense and growl out a long drawn-out "yes".

She spread her legs further and he climbed between them. She took him in hand and drew him to the opening of her body. He eased in a little at a time, making sure she was comfortable. Once he was fully engulfed by her he paused for a moment, to ensure she was ready. She moved a little and then her inner muscles squeezed him, and he started moving, slowly at first, building speed as the sensations increased.

He loved her with long smooth strokes, enjoying every delicious part of her on his most sensitive flesh. It was magnificent. As the feelings grew, she wrapped her legs around his hips, so he slid in a little further and hit a slightly different angle that caused her to gasp in delight.

When he sensed they were both getting close he sped up and increased his thrusts. She clutched his arms and threw her head back with a long groan, his name at the end. Her body milked him, and he joined her in release burying his face in her hair, her name on his lips.

ammy couldn't stop the sappy smile she had on her face for the world. She'd been on cloud nine since the first night with Ted in her bed. He was a magnificent lover. She'd never enjoyed sex as much as she did with him.

The fact that he always made sure to give her a preliminary orgasm before he joined her, and then gave her a second one, certainly had something to do with that. But he was also very inventive. Trying out different positions and… well, if she thought about it anymore, she was going to get turned on, and that just wouldn't do for her shift at work. Then she'd be all itchy for him. Better to nip those thoughts in the bud and do her job, instead of reliving some truly amazing sex.

He was also a cuddler, they'd lay tangled in each other's arms for hours, sharing bits of their lives, stories from the past, hopes for the future, their likes and dislikes. Funny stories and sad ones, they talked and talked until their bodies started to stir, or until they were ready for sleep.

They'd also had fun at various town events, listening to

the carolers, watching the tree lighting, seeing the children in awe of Santa. Long walks through town, window shopping, chatting with friends. They went to the bar and danced, or played pool or darts. Some nights they took a blanket and laid out under the stars, while Ted talked about how he'd envisioned stories in the stars, as a child. It had been the most amazing time of her life.

She was busy at a table of five, the kids bickering over who was the hungriest and the parents studiously ignoring them. When she managed to get their orders and take them to the cook, she came back out to find Ted's mother seated in her section.

Oh, boy. The woman didn't normally frequent the restaurant, unless she was with Ted.

She slapped a regular smile on her face, forcing the sappy one into submission and took the coffee pot over. "Hello, Mrs. Beaumont-Jordan, it's nice to see you here."

Lenore looked up at her with a slight frown on her face. "Are you the one Ted's been spending all his time with?"

"Guilty as charged. He's a great guy."

"Yes, he is."

"Would you like some coffee?"

She looked at the coffee pot Tammy was holding. "Yes, that would be nice."

Tammy filled her coffee cup, waiting for whatever Ted's mother was going to say next. The menu was beneath her carefully folded hands.

"How long have you worked here?"

Tammy thought that was an odd question, but she answered it. "I started here the summer of the big fire."

"So, did you see my son when he came in here?"

"I did, he was a nice boy then, too. A bit on the ragged side, but still nice."

"That's a kind way of putting it. My poor son was nearly

an animal, eating with his hands, thinking a jail cell was luxurious. Dressed in buckskin and moccasins. I shudder to think about it."

Tammy could see where the woman was coming from, but Ted had also been caring and concerned about others. "That's true, but he was a sweet boy even then. He was polite to people and wanted to make sure he wasn't hurting others."

Lenore nodded and wiped a tear away. "He does have a sweet nature. But he's not that boy anymore. He's a man and he's running a multi-billion-dollar company, his net worth is at least a billion, probably more. We're an old family with a successful track record in business."

"Yes, Ted has mentioned running the company."

"So, if you're in this relationship with him for the money—"

Tammy cut her off. "You have nothing to worry about in that area. I like Ted, and it has nothing to do with his money."

"You're a waitress and have been for over a decade, a nice rich man—"

She cut her off again. "I will have my degree in public relations in June and then I plan to open my own PR firm. I have everything I need to do so, set aside. I'm just waiting to graduate. I am not looking for a handout."

"That's good to know. Ted's father married me for my money and when my father didn't hand it over, he stole Ted away from me. I don't want Ted to suffer the same fate."

Tammy felt bad for the woman and her ire died. "I'm sorry you went through that, but I'm enjoying Ted while he's here in town and I have no intention of trying to milk him for money. We both know this is a short-term relationship. You have nothing to worry about. Now I need to get back to work, may I bring you some breakfast?"

"No, thank you, the coffee is fine. I need to get going. Thank you for hearing me out."

Tammy nodded and went to get the family of five's breakfast. She was still fuming over what Ted's mother had thought about her, while on the other hand felt sorry for the woman.

~

TED WAS SURPRISED TO FIND HIS MOTHER HAD LEFT THE HOUSE so early this morning, she normally didn't go out before noon unless she was needed at the firm. He'd thought to devote a few minutes to her today, since he'd been spending so much time with Tammy.

He'd felt bad about leaving his mom alone so much and since Tammy was working until one today, he had the time. He was on his tablet checking on the news and stocks, plus answering a few emails at the breakfast table with a cup of coffee by his elbow, when his mom came in.

He glanced up. "Hello Mother, you've been out early this morning."

She nodded but didn't elaborate and sat at the table with him. "Anything interesting going on?"

"I got an email from the auditor going over the books for year end. He says he found a bit of an anomaly and will get back to me when he tracks it down."

His mother nodded, "That's good."

Good? She hadn't heard a word he'd said. "Mom, is something wrong?"

She startled and looked askance at him. Was that guilt in her eyes? "Oh no Teddy, I'm just thinking about Christmas, there is only a few days left. It will be different having it here in Chedwick."

He chuckled. "Now that's an understatement, but I think it will be a fun change of pace, don't you?"

"What's on the agenda tonight?"

"A hayride. The cattle ranchers have a hayride, we're going at sunset."

She nodded. "It should be very pretty then. There aren't many clouds today."

"Are you thinking about coming to the Christmas Eve reading at the library? Everyone wears Christmas sweaters and Santa hats."

"I have neither of those."

"Which is why I was asking. They have hats in town, but you would have to order a sweater. I'm sure someone would be willing to send one here for a primo price, it's in four days."

"I'll probably skip it. Where would I wear a Christmas sweater?"

"You could donate it to charity after the event."

"True. I'll think about it."

"Think quick," he said with a grin.

CHAPTER TEN

Tammy was excited about the hayride on the Jefferson's ranch today, they'd decided to go at sunset, which in the Pacific Northwest, a few days before Christmas, meant a little after four. The hayrides were scheduled on the hour, but they didn't actually start until ten to fifteen minutes after the scheduled time, to give everyone a chance to get settled on the wagon, and covered up in the warm blankets provided.

They also had homemade hot chocolate, coffee, or hot apple cider to hold and sip. She and Ted were dressed in their winter coats, hats, and gloves, covered in a warm blanket and holding their cups. She'd gone for hot chocolate and he'd chosen the cider.

The horses pulling the wagon—they didn't get enough snow in the valley to use a sleigh—started out slowly, allowing everyone to become accustomed to the movement. The ranch had a gorgeous view of the mountains, and there was a slight hill in one area that had a wonderful view of the lake, so that was the path the ride took.

There was soft Christmas music playing from speakers under the driver's seat. A family of four and one other couple were the other occupants of the wagon, so there was plenty of room for privacy. Ted had one arm wrapped around her, holding her close and held his cup in the other. The view of the lake as the sun set and sent splashes of color across it, was magnificent and they tarried a few moments for everyone to enjoy, before starting back. They didn't take this route once the twilight ended, since the view couldn't be seen in the dark.

They were off the hill and crossing the pasture when Ted's cell phone buzzed, she could feel the vibration, since it was in a pocket next to her. He didn't even try to answer it since his hands were full of her, and his drink.

"Aren't you going to answer that?"

"No, they can leave a message. We'll be back soon enough."

Before they got within sight of the house his phone had gone off two more times. He finally had handed her his cup and taken his arm from around her to answer the cell on the fourth call.

"What is it?" he growled into the phone, clearly not happy about the interruption. He listened for what seemed like a long time.

"Fine, send the jet to Wenatche, and the helicopter to the house. You've already called Mom?"

He nodded. "All right. Good. We'll be there in the morning. Eleven should be fine."

When he got off the phone Tammy noticed a quiet had descended over the hayride, it seemed like everyone had been listening in on his conversation.

Ted turned to her, regret in his eyes, along with a healthy dose of anger. "I'm sorry, Tammy, I'm going to have to cut our evening short. I have to get back for an emergency meeting in the morning. There's been some trouble and mom and I both need to be on hand to deal with it."

She nodded. "You go, take care of your company. Let me know if there is anything I can help with."

"Thanks, I'll do that." He hugged her close as the wagon pulled into the yard, but she sensed he was already across the continent dealing with whatever had gone wrong.

The drive back to her house was done in silence. He'd given her an absent kiss when he'd walked her to the door, and had promised to be back as soon as possible. She wanted to, but didn't, believe him. He was already lost to her.

TED WAS FUMING. SIX DAMN WEEKS, ALL HE'D ASKED FOR WAS six weeks. But no, four days before Christmas and he had to return for an emergency board meeting, which would likely result in him having to fire his CFO. Embezzlement. Shit. Why couldn't people be satisfied with their pay, and it they weren't, couldn't they just ask for a raise? Stealing was wrong and everyone knew it.

Everyone except people like his father, that is. He didn't want to think about his father. Ted had even realized on some level that it was wrong, when he'd been burnt out of his home, and had stolen to survive. Which is why he'd left the carvings at the art gallery. He'd certainly not learned those morals from dear old dad, they'd been instinctual.

How someone could deliberately embezzle from a company he just didn't understand. He supposed he'd hear excuses soon. Ted wasn't a fan of confrontation, but in this case, he felt like firing the guy just for making him come back. He didn't want to leave Chedwick. He wanted to be back with Tammy in his arms, drinking hot chocolate or making love, even just walking around town and window shopping, would be better than hauling his ass clear across the country to deal with a thief.

He vowed to make this a quick trip and be back in a day or two at most.

Tammy had to pull herself together. She'd been depressed for nearly four days. Every time she spotted the gift she'd gotten for Ted; the water works had started up. She'd considered throwing it in the trash, so it wasn't in her view, but couldn't manage to do it.

She'd been so excited to buy it for him and had wrapped it with loving care. She didn't have a lot of people she exchanged gifts with. She had no family anymore. She bought a gift for Amber and a couple of her girlfriends but nothing much, so adding Ted's to her meager gifts had made her so happy, until he'd taken off four days ago, now it made her sad.

She didn't think she would ever give it to him. She didn't believe he'd be back to Chedwick. He'd texted her a couple of times saying everything was a mess. He'd called her once to ask for suggestions on the PR side of things, but he'd been so stiff and formal, she'd known then, that their relationship was over and done with.

Tammy still couldn't remove his gift from under her tree.

She dragged herself to the shower, she was going to the

library for the Christmas Eve story telling whether she felt like it or not. It was tradition, not a very old tradition, since the previous library hadn't had the room for anything like that, but a tradition just the same.

After she'd showered and dried her hair, she pulled on her new Christmas sweater. The tradition included everyone wearing a Christmas sweater and Santa hat. Her new sweater was white with red poinsettia accents and polka dots.

She joined the throngs of others all heading toward the library. It was a little bit of a walk since it was outside of town, but walking with everyone else made it seem quick. After the story telling and snacks, there would be people shuttling everyone back to town.

Everyone slowed as they reached the library. The town peacock was standing next to the entry, with his tail feathers unfurled for all to see. Tammy was surprised to see him and wondered why he was there. He rarely was seen around town unless some significant event was taking place, as far as she knew the book reading had never attracted him. As she walked past, he seemed to be watching her, she was startled by the effect his attention on her generated. Then she decided she was being foolish and figured everyone felt the same with his beady eyes on them.

She settled into a cozy corner with a couple of friends and prepared to listen to the story. Just as Patty Anne picked up the book to read, the door whooshed open bringing in a cold blast of air. She turned toward the door and was surprised to see Ted walk in, he was unshaven and looked exhausted, but he had on a red Christmas sweater and a Santa hat.

When he spotted her a smile covered his face and he walked directly to her, glanced up and drew her less than a yard to the right. Then he kissed her with enough passion to set the room on fire. They had never kissed in public, so she was startled by his action, but not enough to cancel the enjoyment of being in his arms with his mouth on hers.

Her blood was boiling, her knees weak, and her head was spinning when he pulled back. She couldn't form a word let alone a coherent question, but her expression must have said it all. He grinned at her and pointed up. "Blame the mistletoe."

She looked up and yes, directly above her head, was a small sprig of mistletoe.

Patty Anne cleared her voice. "Welcome back Ted, now if we could all turn our attention toward me, I will begin the reading."

Tammy and Ted both turned toward the librarian, but Tammy didn't hear a single word she said. Ted was back.

TED WAS SO GLAD TO BE BACK IN CHEDWICK WITH TAMMY IN his arms, he didn't care if the reading was out of The Shining. He tried to listen, but the feel of Tammy in his arms was better than anything else he could imagine. She belonged there, in his arms, now he needed to figure out a way to convince her.

After the reading, and everyone greeting him, he and Tammy decided to walk back to town. It was a cold clear night and he wanted to look at his woman under the stars, the moon was bright even though it was only about half, the full moon wouldn't be for another few days.

They walked hand in hand, both wore gloves, but he still enjoyed the contact. He'd missed her so damn bad while he'd been off fixing things. It had taken days, rather than the hours he'd first predicted. But everything was on target now. He'd had to fire most of his accounting team, they'd all been in on the embezzlement.

"I missed you, Tammy. I couldn't wait to get back here."

She said softly, "I thought you were gone for good."

"Why would you think that? I said I'd be back."

She shrugged and didn't look at him. "Tammy, talk to me."

She drew in a shuddery breath, and he wished they were somewhere with more light, so he could see her face. "I didn't hear from you much, and the one time you did call you were so cold and formal. I thought you were over me."

"Oh, sweetheart, no. I was in the middle of a board meeting where I had insisted you would have good advice. I didn't tell you at the time, because I didn't want you to be nervous and clam up, but I had you on speaker phone. So, I had to be more formal."

"Speaker phone?" She screeched. "Yeah, that was probably a good call not telling me. Did I sound like an idiot?"

"Not at all, you gave us good advice that we implemented. In fact, my board said they would like to get your input in other areas and told me to put you on a retainer."

She stopped and looked up at him. "Seriously?"

"Absolutely. So, if you'll take us, you have your first client."

She grinned, then frowned. "This isn't some kind of pity thing, or you taking care of your girlfriend, is it?"

He shook his head. "No, not at all. The board all voted on it and gave me a suggested amount to keep you on."

She grinned. "My first client, and I haven't even graduated yet."

"You better get yourself a business license and bank account immediately."

"I'll do that first thing tomorrow. Well, not tomorrow, but the first day the bank and city offices are open."

CHAPTER TWELVE

Tammy thought she might faint from the amount Ted had casually mentioned they planned to pay her as a retainer. She had her first client, all right, and it was a whopper.

They were back in town and to her house, by the time her head stopped spinning. When she invited him in, he agreed quickly. Once they were inside, he took her arm and steered her into the living room. She'd thought to go straight to the bedroom, but he had other ideas.

They stripped out of their winter gear and he pulled her to the couch.

He took her hand in his and rubbed his thumb over her knuckles. "Tammy, I'm sorry I didn't call you more often, the hours we put in getting everything straightened out were long and draining. Every day before we started and after we finished, I thought of calling you, but the time difference made the hours crazy, so I didn't. I didn't know what work schedule you were on, or what activities you might be doing in town. I didn't want to interrupt your life."

"Ted, I didn't do much of anything, but yearn for your

call. I would have been happy to talk to you at two in the morning."

"I'll remember that next time."

"Next time?"

"Yes. I love you, Tammy, and I want to spend a lot more time together."

"But we live on opposite sides of the country."

"Do you want to spend more time with me?" he asked softly.

"Yes. I love you too, Ted."

The smile that covered his face was magnificent. "Then the rest is just logistics. My jet and helicopter and their pilots will be putting in more hours."

She laughed and drew him to his feet. "Let's go celebrate our love."

"One more thing." He shuffled his feet. "Will you come to my house for brunch tomorrow? I'd like you and my mom to get better acquainted too."

She shuddered at the idea, his mom didn't like her very much, but if she wanted to see more of Ted, she needed to try to make friends with his mom.

She smiled up at him. "Yes, I will. Anything else?"

"No, thanks for agreeing to come to brunch."

"Of course, now let's go revel in our love for each other."

He swooped her up in his arms and carried her to the bedroom. "Gladly."

They spent the night in each other's arms, rejoicing in the love they shared. Enjoying each other's body, making slow sweet love, after the first bout of wild crazed sex. They'd missed each other too badly to go slow at first. He'd left before dawn, saying he'd see her again in a few hours. She fell back to sleep a smile on her lips and joy in her heart.

~

Ted paced the foyer, waiting for Tammy to arrive, she wasn't due for another ten minutes, but he couldn't settle.

His mother joined him, "Teddy, why are you so nervous?"

He shrugged. "I want you and her to like each other. I love her, Mom."

"That's been fairly obvious, darling. Do you plan to marry her?"

"I want to."

"Do you think she'll fit into the society we live in?"

"She fits me, so if I can fit in, so can she. She won't be catty and rude like many of the other women. That's one of the things I love about her. She accepted me as a scruffy boy eating with my hands, and she accepts me as the business-man. She's kind and good, like you are, Mom."

"I wasn't always that way. I could be snotty in my younger days, not as difficult as Rebecca... But hardships mellow a person. So many of the people that helped me during those difficult times after you were taken from me, were not the society I was accustomed to. The society was indifferent toward me and my pain. Some of them even thought I deserved it, for marrying someone not from our class."

Ted hugged his mother, not knowing anything else to do.

"The police officers, and social workers, and counselors, those were the people with compassion. They weren't from our social class, but they are the ones that helped me, cared for me. If you want to marry her, I will accept your choice and welcome her into our family."

He hugged his mother and kissed her cheek. "That's all I could ask."

The doorbell rang and Ted bolted to answer the door. Leaving his mother smiling after him.

With a jerk on the handle he yanked the door open, and there on the porch stood his girl. He ushered her in and took her coat and gloves, and the gift bag from her hands. She had on a pretty red dress with white reindeer frolicking on the cuffs and hem of the skirt. She looked amazing and he gave her a quick kiss, right in front of his mother.

She blushed a delightful shade of pink. While he hung up her coat, she greeted his mom, cordial and sweet, as she always was. They went to the family room where the furniture was comfortable, rather than formal. The tree was large, and gifts surrounded the bottom. Ted put her gift bag by the tree. There were fancy hors d'oeuvres on a coffee table.

Ted said, "Can I get you a drink, Tammy? We have eggnog, with or without alcohol, mimosas, bloody Mary's, hot chocolate, regular cocktails…"

Tammy said, "A mimosa would be perfect."

He grinned at her, and stepped to a small wet bar tucked into a corner. He brought both his mother and his girlfriend a mimosa. He had water.

They had a few of the snacks and engaged in small talk.

After the meal of ham and turkey, meatballs in gravy and a dozen side dishes, Ted announced that it was gift opening time. So, they all went back to the family room where Ted put the Santa hat on and started delivering gifts.

Tammy was surprised as Ted put gift after gift in her lap. She had no idea what they could possibly be or why he'd gone so crazy. He looked very excited to have a gift from her. Tammy had also found a gift for his mother.

As she opened her gifts, she realized she'd been duped the day they'd gone to the art gallery. He'd bought her each of the things she'd admired, while he was asking her 'opinion' on gifts for his mother. Earrings, a set of her favorite fragrance of the body lotion, shampoo and other products, made by the woman in town from wildflowers in the valley.

One of his sculptures that she'd adored, and a half dozen other items.

There were a few gifts for Lenora from the gallery but not nearly as many as Tammy had. The stinker.

Ted saved the gift from Tammy until last. When he opened it, he swallowed hard as if fighting tears. It was a picture of a meadow filled with flowers, some of them the ones in the lotion he'd purchased her.

He looked up at her and smiled a soft smile. "It looks like the meadow I played in as a child." He turned toward his mom. "I used to dream of you, my Angel, meeting me in the meadow. We had long talks and played games."

His mother's mouth made and O shape but nothing came out, and she dabbed at tears.

"Thank you, Tammy. It's perfect."

Lenore put the soft cashmere scarf Tammy had given her around her neck. "I love my gift, too. Thank you, Tammy."

"And thank you both for so many wonderful gifts."

Ted cleared his throat and she saw him wipe his palms on his slacks. "I have one more for you, Tammy."

"Oh, no, you've given me too much already."

"This one comes with a question." He came over and knelt in front of her. "I know it's only been a few weeks, but I know in my heart that you are my one and only. Tamara Janine Lynch, will you make me the happiest man on earth by becoming my wife?"

The breath backed up in her throat and she squeaked out. "Really?"

He smiled, "Yes Tammy. I love you and I want to be with you, always. Will you marry me, fly back and forth from coast to coast with me, have my babies, counsel my company, but mostly, be my love?"

Tears had pooled in her eyes and she blinked so she could see his handsome face clearly. "Yes, Theodore Gerald Beaumont-Jordan, I would love to marry you. I think I've loved you since you were a boy in buckskins, eating your salad with your hands, and handing handfuls of money to Amber to pay for a ten-dollar lunch."

He laughed and handed her a gift box with a bright red bow on top. She opened it to find the most beautiful engagement ring she'd ever seen. He slid it on her finger, it was a perfect fit. "How did you know… oh, all those rings you had me try on, that day at the art gallery. Sneaky."

He nodded. "Caught me."

And she had, she marveled at the fact that she, a small-town girl, had caught the most wonderful man in the world.

ew Year's Eve at Greg's bar was a festive event. Nearly every adult from town was squished together in the limited space. Most of the tables and chairs had been cleared to make more room. There was no dart playing or pool games, there wasn't room for those activities.

If they got near one of the speakers, they could hear music coming from them, but three feet away it was drowned out by the chatter. Tammy talked with her friends and neighbors, introducing Ted to a few he'd not met yet.

She'd not mentioned her engagement to most of them, only her closest friends, and Amber, so she could begin looking for a replacement for Tammy. She didn't think Ted was going to leave her in Chedwick when he had to go back to the other side of the country, or to some foreign land.

In the few days between Christmas and New Year's Eve they'd applied for a passport for her. Packed up most of her belongings and had told the real estate agent she would be vacating her little apartment.

As midnight drew near, they found themselves in front by

the bar. Ted nodded at Greg who whistled and got everyone's attention. Tammy was surprised at the dead silence that came over the bar, not a word was spoken. Greg said, "Before midnight arrives, Ted has an announcement."

Ted hopped up on a barstool. "I just wanted to thank all of you, for the parts you have played in my life. From not prosecuting me for stealing from some of you, when I was a kid that didn't know any better, to accepting me as a friend and neighbor. I appreciate everything, more than you can possibly imagine."

Several people called out, and others laughed or cheered. Ted got them to quiet down again. "I'm going to repay your kindness by stealing from you again. Not stuff, I can afford my own things now, and actually know how to use money… and a fork."

People laughed and Ted grinned.

When he started speaking again silence reigned. "I'm stealing one of your favorite people. She's so sweet and kind, I know you're going to miss her generous smile, so I vow to come back often, maybe not half the year, but as often as we can. Friends and family, please join me in my joy. Your Tammy Lynch has agreed to become my wife."

Cheers filled the bar and Tammy was pulled up to stand next to Ted. The cheers turned to chants of Kiss, Kiss, Kiss. So, he kissed her, and more cheers erupted. A few minutes later midnight struck and there were kisses throughout the bar, followed by noisemakers and toasts.

Tammy caught a glimpse of Ted's mother in a dark corner, kissing the guy that worked at the pharmacy. She pointed it out to Ted, who said, "Blame the mistletoe."

And Tammy saw that Lenore Beaumont-Jordan had a sprig of mistletoe nestled in her hair. She laughed and whispered, "I guess your mom will be happy to return, any time."

Then she kissed her fiancé. They didn't need mistletoe as an excuse, they had love and it was much more powerful.

THE END

62

LAKE CHELAN SERIES

First Responders

The Rancher's Lady: A Lake Chelan novella

Hank and Ellen's story

Sawdust and Satin: Lake Chelan #1

Chris and Barbara's story

Designs on Her: Lake Chelan #2

Nolan and Kristen's story

Smokin': Lake Chelan #3

Jeremy and Amber's story

Fire on the Mountain: Lake Chelan #4

Trey and Mary Ann's story

The Fire Chief's Desire: Lake Chelan #5

Greg and Sandy's story

Mysterious Ways: Lake Chelan #6

Scott and Nicole's story

Conflict of Interest: Lake Chelan #7

David and Jacqueline's story

Another Chance for Love: Lake Chelan #8

Max and Carol's story

Frames: Lake Chelan #9

Terry and Deborah's story

Christmas in Lake Chelan: Lake Chelan #10

Ted and Tammy's story

BURLAP AND BARBED WIRE SERIES

Colorado Cowboys

A Cowboy for Alyssa: Burlap and Barbed Wire #1

Beau and Alyssa's story

Taming Adam: Burlap and Barbed Wire #2

Adam and Rachel's story

Tempting Chase: Burlap and Barbed Wire #3

Chase and Katie's story

Roping Cade: Burlap and Barbed Wire #4

Cade and Summer's story

Trusting Drew: Burlap and Barbed Wire #5

Drew and Lily's story

Emma's Rodeo Cowboy: Burlap and Barbed Wire #6

Emma and Zach's story

SADDLES AND SECRETS SERIES

Wyoming Wranglers

The Lawman: Saddles and Secrets #1

Maggie Ann and John's story

The Watcher: Saddles and Secrets #2

Christina and Rob's story

The Rescuer: Saddles and Secrets #3

Milly and Tim's story

The Vacation: Saddles and Secrets Short Story

Andrea and Carl Ray's story

(Part of the Getting Wild in Deadwood anthology)

STAND ALONE

Helluva Engineer

Patricia and Steve's story

What does a geeky math nerd know about writing romance?

That's a darn good question. As a former techy I've done everything from computer programming to international trainer. Prior to college I had lots of different jobs and activities that were so diverse, I was an anomaly.

None of that qualifies me for writing novels. But I have some darn good stories to tell and a lot of imagination.

I have lived in Colorado, Hawaii and currently reside in Washington. Going from two states with 340 days of sun to a state with 340 days of clouds, I had to do something to perk me up. And that's when I started this new adventure called author. Joining the Romance Writers of America and two local chapters, helped me learn the craft quickly and was a ton of fun.

My family consists of two grown children, their spouses, two adorable grand-daughters, and one grand dog. My favorite activity is playing with my granddaughters!

When the girls can't play with their amazing grandmother, my interests are reading and writing, yay! I started reading at a young age with the Nancy Drew mysteries and have continued to be an avid reader my whole life. My favorite reading material is romance, but occasionally if other stories creep into my to-be-read pile, I don't kick them out.

Some of the strange jobs I have held are a carnation grower's worker, a trap club puller, a pizza hut waitress, a software engineer, an international trainer, and a business program manager. I took welding, drafting and upholstery in high school, a long time ago, when girls didn't take those classes, so I have an eclectic bunch of knowledge and experience.

And for something really unusual… I once had a raccoon as a pet.

Join with me as I tell my stories, weaving real tidbits from my life in with imaginary ones. You'll have to guess which is which. It will be a hoot!

Contact me:

www.shirleypenick.com

To sign up for Shirley's Monthly Newsletter, sign up on my website or send email to shirleypenick@outlook.com, subject newsletter.

Follow me:

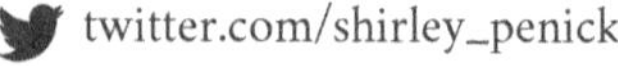

facebook.com/ShirleyPenickAuthorFans

twitter.com/shirley_penick

instagram.com/shirleypenickauthor

bookbub.com/authors/shirley-penick